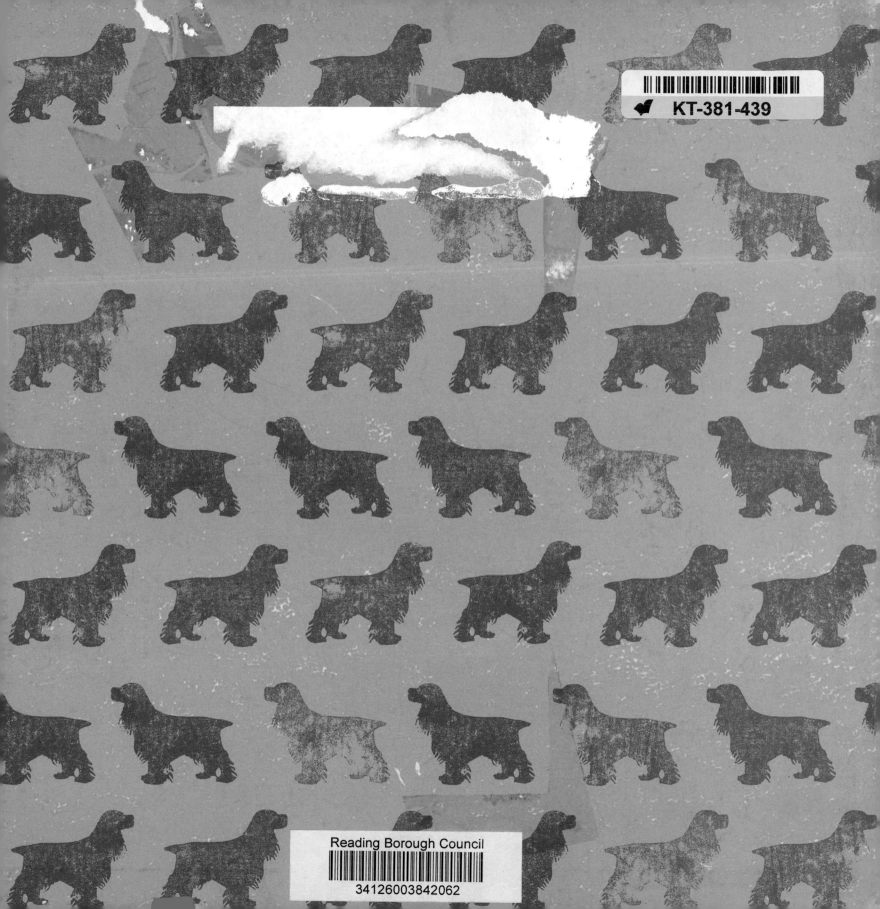

For May, Max, Beth, Osca
and dog lovers everywhere! — H.S.

JANETTA OTTER-BARRY BOOKS

First published in Great Britain in 2016 by
Frances Lincoln Children's Books, 74-77 White Lion Street, London N1 9PF
QuartoKnows.com
Visit our blogs at QuartoKnows.com

Text and illustrations copyright © Holly Sterling 2016
The right of Holly Sterling to be identified as the author and illustrator
of this work has been asserted by her in accordance with the
Copyright, Designs and Patents Act, 1988 (United Kingdom).

A CIP catalogue record for this book is available from the British Library.

ISBN 978-1-84780-674-1

Illustrated with watercolour, pencil and 'printed' textures.

Printed in China

1 3 5 7 9 8 6 4 2

Hiccups!

Holly Sterling

Frances Lincoln
Children's Books

One morning Ruby and Oscar were playing
their favourite game, when all of a sudden...

"Oh dear, Oscar!" said Ruby.
"How are we going to get rid of those hiccups?"

"I know, why don't we try **dancey-dancing** like this?"
said Ruby.

Hic!

Oscar danced just like Ruby, but the hiccups did not stop.

"How about if we jumpity-jump like this?" said Ruby.
Oscar jumped just like Ruby, but the hiccups were still there.

Hic!

"What if we **slurpity-slurp** like this?" said Ruby.

Oscar slurped through his straw,
but that didn't work either.

They **munchy-munched**

Hic!

and **tickly-tickled**

Hic!

but NOTHING could make Oscar's hiccups disappear!

Ruby stopped to think.

"Aha!" she said.
"I know exactly what will
get rid of your hiccups."

Ruby went to her toy box in search of her...

magic wand and wizard's hat.
With a *swish* and a *swoosh* she waved her wand.

Ruby threw her wand to the ground and tried a very loud

stompity-stomp instead.

But...

Oscar just could not stop!

Then Ruby had a really BRILLIANT idea.

She ran away and came back
wearing her special furry...

dress-up cat costume!

"Meeeoooow!"

she shouted.

Oscar was a bit scared!
His ears blew back and his tail
gave a very small wiggle-waggle...

but he DIDN'T hiccup!

"They've gone!" said Ruby. "Your hiccups have gone!"
And she gave Oscar a great big hug.

"Woof! Woof!" barked Oscar.

Feeling very pleased with themselves, Ruby and Oscar went back to playing their favourite game,

until all of a sudden...